the requiem zoar

the requiem zoar

v regi weile

photography by
nancy muller
ingeborg tallarek

ZKHUT WORDSMITH

ISBN 13 978-0615966175

Library of Congress Control Number 201 4910380

ZKHUT WORDSMITH
p.o. box 223
east marion
new york 11939

zkhutwordsmith@gmail.com

Editorial Consultant Thomas DeWolfe

Book and Cover design by Kim Shkapich

This work was inspired by John and Gloria Hejduk
...finding them woven in the World's protective cloth of souls, warp upon weft.

exordium

Journeys, imaginary portraits of inquiry, recur hauntingly in quests for the place for Truth's aspirated breath of language, believed to be sealed within a city of refuge named Zoar.

One asks What is this about? in order to affirm the exigency of the narratable journey. The earthly author responds to the question, turning it around to ask, *Who* is this about?

A *Narrator* sets out upon a journey in search of a city or place of refuge, chronicling stories heard as landscapes pass through them.

The Narrator has a *Companion*, who serves as a sieve, sifting the pedagogical lessons of wakefulness and dreaming from stories found along the way. As places pass through stories, the stories, by accommodation, drift in bias and are altered: A flood, in a story, as *alluvial*, is an affirmer of life, as opposed to a *cataclysmic deluge*, which is an extinguisher of life. The Companion reveals these modulations to the Narrator as a teller of vision, as would an inner voice to a questioning mind.

Natura, who gifted the world its landscape uncontaminated, untouched and unspoiled by human intervention, accommodates their trespass.

Aspirants and their junior *Initiates* follow a quest similar to that of the Narrator. They seek a place of refuge, having found the general ideas upon which the world is based unacceptable, and set out in search of alternatives. A place of refuge, but one that differs from the Narrator's in its requisite of disencumbrance of responsibility.

Children, for whom companionship is the refuge, thrive on the sounds of the stories.

A *Recluse* finds the place of refuge within herself and is enabled to proclaim freedom from the restraints of emblematic religion, social and symbolic ritual. She is her own place and becomes a beacon to those who follow.

vrw

1

emigratus [1]

My journey, a lingering emigratus, began some time ago. It was a quest, a search for the gravity that draws out life's breath, revealing the unity of nature with conscious life. Walking in a westerly direction, I traveled at varying paces, following a landscape littered with stories of things heard and imagined existence. The stories' threads intertwined in weavings of a vaguely perceptible fabric, woven warp upon weft as longitude upon latitude, setting place on an imagined geographic plane. My pace was slackened where intricacies and speculation were valued and hastened where the sciences were esteemed. These stories formed the voice of a fellow traveler and companion.

Stories emigrate, as do songs and poetry. Imagination is their wit. They observe, they witness, so as to authenticate. They combine such things as perception with expression, the incongruous with the related, the believable with the unbelievable, and journey with a thirst for renewal. At each new place they absorb, they accept restoration. They do not pass through a place and move on, it is more as if the place passes through them, restoring them, rewriting them, giving them new fullness. They are Ozick's pilgrims.

Stories move as the elements, freely and fruitfully, move with the disorder of intellect, as intellect freed of syntax. They move without consideration of actuality as located before or after observation. Their language is filled with metaphors that reveal, that also hide, a peculiar madness. What else could come from a mixture of the believable with the unbelievable, of the possible with the impossible.…

As places pass through the stories, a residue is impressed upon the landscape. It is as if the stories were given flesh, bones and muscle that are shed, shed and strewn upon the earth, residue forming boundaries, skeletonized icons and geographic markers, left for a time after, left as physical image vacated by the aural mind.

On occasion, the residue is given new substance, fleshed out, translated into material form, casting light and shadow upon the expanse. This is the work of Artificers, speaking in the language of stone, of brick and of mortar. Their fabrications have a formidable presence and, unlike common recitation, challenge time and sensibility in resounding monumentality of ideas substantiated.

The location and construction of an Artifice is determined by survey in the application of geometry. Although a simple science, geometry fell, along with other supreme tenets, under a cloak of mystery. It fell under the jurisdiction of a select lineage, which began with Thoth, the Egyptian Hermes, who was able to decipher, then absorb, the continuous magnitudes of geometric tracings of sacred script from the ether above. To absorb, then to transform the tracings into a model from which to copy. These geometries, poised above in readiness, offered the potential to pollinate the mind and inspire the hand.

> The Egyptians ate the flesh of enemy warriors to gain the
> dead warriors strength. Ingestion as cannibalism.

> The Artificers absorbed the ethereal geometries of sky-bound
> script to substantiate form. Ingestion as fertilization.

The supreme tenet of the Artificer was unspeakable. By inference alone it was passed from mentor to novice, insuring unification of the imagined with the real. The Artificer formed strongholds against challenges of the immense, the unknowable, and at times even against reason. Piercing the sky, they pierced the earth with equal vigor, by implication of the maxim of the mystery of the hermetic axiom:

> *That which is below is as that which is above, and that which
> is above is as that which is below, for the performance of the
> Miracle of the One Thing.*[2]

To look only at the apparent image, the one above, was to look without the mind. At the intersection of that which appeared above and that assumed below, barnacle-like forms spread geometrically outward, embracing the Artifice and at the same time pulling away from it. Pulling as a tent peg driven into the earth's surface pulls away from that of which it is the sole support. These formations, resonating with potential energy, had the appearance of corporeal shadows.

2

the seed-bearer

My companion met each place as fruitful soil meets the seed. I met each place hoping to "bind sheaves of favor in fields of fear and retribution."[3]
Who are you? I was asked upon approach. In the most Adamic gesture I named myself. I am a visitor.
And whence do you come?

> From the East.

And to what destination do you travel?

> I travel West, as all humanity before me.

And what do you carry?

> A weary body, a staff and lantern's light. I bring stories, a
> companion, a thirst for seeing and hearing accompanied by
> the need for replenishment so that I may continue my journey.

What was it they saw clutched in my hand? A scythe of death to cut life down, a shepherd's crook by which to lead men or a torch of wasteful light known to be carried by the angel of darkness? Or was it only a probe in the hand of a wanderer, a simple staff to guide one unknown through the unknowable?

I am a visitor, I repeated. I have come from the East. I am traveling West. I bring the path of a weary body, and stories. Speech is my companion and kinsman.

Speech fitted close unites us, binding our thought. It wards off and averts the burden of circumstance. It is a cave that shields and a necessary cloak that conceals the imperfections of its wearer. Draped as a monk's habit, a rabbi's shawl, a cardinal's vestment, it is bound by threads tied or woven in amuletic knots.

Presenting myself as incapable of merging men into mass, I was able to defer judgment and avoid the error of mistaken identity, that of being mistaken for a stranger. When approaching new places, it was always with the understanding of the subtle difference between a *visitor* and a *stranger*.

Cordiality meets the visitor, superstition the stranger. Visitors are invited into the home, strangers only to the door. The duration of the visitor's stay is temporary, of the stranger unknown. To be a visitor is social; to be a stranger, political. Strangers suffer a vulnerability from which the visitor is exempted. History, legend and myth have assured this.

Sargon the Second was responsible for the invention of *strangers* when he set a precedent for the shifting about of whole populations. Beginning with the deportation of the ten tribes, whole nations in times past and not so past were wrenched from their homes en masse and sent to hostile and unaccustomed regions as strangers, having as their only hope of survival obedience to that which was most foreign to them. Those to whose doors they came knocking feared them as emissaries of the angel of darkness, set upon them to disrupt an imagined pride of redemption.

3

it is of yourself that the tale is told [4]

Traveling a great distance I found that the stories, or something learned from them, were leading me to a specific place. I was not sure in what sense this place existed. Each story revealed clues as to its presence but not its location. As I moved along in one direction my path seemed clear, seemed almost to affirm my journey. When changing direction or testing other signposts, the connecting threads were sometimes lost and a chaotic sensation impeded my progress.

Determined to find the place, I constructed diagrams, mapping what I believed to be above and below its surface. I assumed hypothetical backgrounds and datum for imagined foregrounds which led to the generation of underground and figure-ground. The generated configurations became challenging propositions. With simple geometry I attempted the definition of its layers. Shadows were projected, reflections inverted only to be cast back upon its surface.

As the diagrams grew, parts fell out while others steadfastly remained, forming the space of geometric trance. The more that was known of the place, the smaller and more precise it became. As the stories hinted of possible inhabitants, the diagrams were adjusted to receive them. Some inhabitants could be absorbed, others could not. Some designated and inhabited a center, some saw a center, others were blinded by it while still others aspired to meet it.

The non-miscible of the inhabitants radiated onto an exterior circle of influence. They implemented the materialization of *axis mundi* in order to remain within a communal context. The *axis mundi*, a multitude of symbolic markers, totems of centrality, represented the idea of a center of a universe. The idea of and not an actual center as an accepted reminder of the singularity of origins and diversity of perception.

As one center did not exist, theorems of the concave and convex, curved surfaces that marked limits of inside and out, were absent. This boundaryless landscape revealed the need for a place in which to tether the inner gyroscopic motion of the soul. The yearning for a place from which to secure momentum was manifested as a quest for a refuge.

I had read somewhere that at a crossroad in the desert the ghosts of all disappeared cities met. Among them I hoped to find this place of refuge. In the midst of a parched and littered desert landscape, among the detritus of collective memory, I recognized its towers, fringed with a fence of stone.

4

earth's false dreams [5]

A desert is always flat. Its surface presses against the heated mass of air that is expanded and illuminated. Its light intensifies with the heat and presses downward, tempting stability.

A desert is always flat. Its light meets the eye now as a plane, now as a wall. Its edge, its horizon, eludes the foot and cannot be overtaken. The cognitive mind, in its anguish, projects the desert's antithesis, the oasis, as the air opens a yawn, revealing the illusion of water.

Walls appeared along the parched horizon, much as ships or their phantoms unexpectedly drift onto vacancy growing out of mere specks. Walls appeared and then towers.

It was a little place, known everywhere although no longer by name. Pronounced by my companion, re-uttered into existence, she emerged from her dormancy.

> *Behold now, this city is near to flee unto, and is a little one.*
> *Oh, let me escape thither is it not a little one, and my soul shall live.* [7]

> *The name of the city was Zoar.*
>
> Genesis 19.21-23

Walls appeared and then towers in their surrounding embrace. The walls were of brick. I perceived this then to be a city of men, built of bricks laid layer upon layer, the work of the hand. The walls, enfolding the stone towers, were poised in a gesture of protection. The stone, cut from the immortal body of creation, was placed by the eternal power of thought, with laws governing nature's defiance. The walls, of handmade and mortal brick, clasped the stone towers firmly, laying claim to the precedence of desired immortality.

The walls taking form before me sporadically opened dark gulfs revealing concentrations of moist air. These wavering concentrations of moisture brought to mind the world of ancient sea gods. A world the mind filled with the memory of the primitive struggle out of the water and onto land. The memory of evolving from the water of the womb coupled with the knowledge that we still breath through water by means of the lung, a fossil of fish-life pressed into our chests, closest to the heart.[8] The stories that led me here told of this moist air, and of the life it holds. Free and unencumbered by matter and invested not only in cells of the living, it also gave life to those cells.

My pace forward did not slacken. I breathed into the ether and its dampness while focusing on the upward projections of vertical resilience. The walls were dry-set with timbers placed as horizontal reinforcement. No sign of siege by the battering ram was apparent. Some walls stood as fortification. Others formed arches embracing underlying entries frozen in poses of feminine gymnastic grace. Gates were revealed, and, like bracelets, enhanced the face of the wall. Other entries were folded between portions of the wall at overlaps. From a distance they were lost to the eye in deep shadows. Reaching a place where the wall opened, an arbor of roses appeared, beckoning me to enter. The arbor appeared, then passed behind me. Walking through this rose embrasure I entered Zoar and with the same ease it entered me.

I found I was in a place that was either within the wall or was the wall itself. There were roses and lilies within iris-lined paths that led in a direction I thought to be west. It was a place that was not quite like Eden or the planted fields of Noah ten generations later. Eden had exempted knowledge and wisdom; Noah's fields exempted the past, held only beginnings and uncertain futurity. Zoar's terra bore witness to a particular unity that carried infinity before and beyond. It was sown with eternal seed that would not ravage time but rather form an ox-goad, a bridge, urging life forward.

My companion, reading from signified textures of the masonry coursework, narrated the passage through the wall. Each course contained a multitude of recognizable textural gestures aligned and punctuated with mortar. The narration revealed stories that were similar to those of a cosmogonic genesis but reversed. Preparation for illumination's ascent to light, wisdom and natural truth were turned backward towards a oneness devoid of division's aspiration.

My companion expounded upon a progressive eradication of divisions. Divisions that were lessened, dissipated, finally absented. What had been divided was joined. First eradicated were the divisions between brothers, between men and women, race and race, wise and ignorant, elders and the innocent. Humanity in its enhancing differentiations merged into homogeneity.

The narrative continued with the separation between the five senses and its consequential effect on animate and inanimate matter. Animate matter differed from the inanimate in nothing other than sensation. The sensations' divisions were fivefold and stood as guardians of the soul. With retraction of the senses' divisions, sensations merged and acuity was diminished. The soul withdrew. In the order of which they partook of soul things animate disappeared. The loss of the senses and the consequent diminishing presence of the soul caused the awakened mind to return to its slumber. In its slumber it had no need of the mouth, the eye, the ear, the nose, or the hand; it had no need to act, to measure, to name or form.

Light and darkness, never equal in their eternal struggle for preeminence, had always managed a palpable balance. Light was ever able to diffuse and penetrate the deepest darkness, even though darkness had failed to touch the purest sphere of light. The smallest amount of light could penetrate and conquer the darkness, while that of equal darkness could never penetrate the light. Now, my companion related, light and darkness in an unrelenting ecliptic embrace merged, causing the sun, moon and stars to lose their individual domains. Their perpetual display of signs communicating a bond between the finite and infinite was lost. The timeless trek of the sun and moon, one in pursuit of the other across the sky, was not to be seen again. Divisions of time were bridged. Time merged into the moment,

a moment, as light fled darkness, and darkness light, as warmth aban-
doned the chilled darkness.

The unembellished vault of heaven, raised to support the sky, displayed
its modest nakedness and was replaced by a tin semi-sphere. The tin fell
away leaving a thin void in its place. In the cold darkness the fertile em-
bellishments of the earth could no longer survive. They dwindled in number,
they bore no fruit. Without fruit there was no seed and all beginnings ended.

Natura cried out to the waters to shield her. The land and the sea opened
their lips to one another and let flow the chaos of antiquity.[9]

Natura, embraced, enveloped in the flow, vanished.

Confused by the watery chaos, the narrative continued; all divisions of
creation lost their boundaries and merged into an abyss. There was
silence. There was a word. The word was retracted. Nothingness prevailed.
Nothingness that contained anticipation.

There was silence. The journey now belonged to memory, its markers and
detritus strewn across the landscape.

5

gilgals [10] ciphers

Encumbered by an addled solemnity, my journey continued. No outward signs aided my orientation or priority as I walked tentatively forward, listening for my companion. For some time I wandered oblivious to goal, reviving, retelling myself, the countless stories heard.

Distraction led me to a field in which I discovered five wells. Each well was of different construction but each contained liquid that reflected images external to it. Looking into each of the wells I saw my image hanging upside down, as if hung by the feet downward into another muted world.

From one well I drew the sweetest water. The second caught my eye with unusual colors and patterns. The internal springs of the next released gurgling sounds that soothed as a lullaby. The next was scented with a freshness that I had never dreamed possible and allowed me to understand the craving for the open sea. The last was impenetrably mercurial. The wells had been generous in their reflections, not distorting beyond inversion, and for this I was grateful.

Eve had found her reflection in a well, a reflection more beautiful than the one she was sentenced to find in the black wells of Adam's eyes. Her reflection was so clear, so brilliant, that it deafened her to Adam's call. That watery reflection, mirroring her image, was to be lost to her forever:

> *Eve bowed her head before Adam. Her second, her outer voice proclaimed,*
> *"Not my will, but thine." Her first and inner voice protested.*
> *"My will is illusive but it is free although hidden, it is reflected and inverted by the mask of thy will."* [11]

In reparation for Eve's loss, water took on the characteristics of a liquid unmiscible with mercury. It was for that reason that man gave woman the mirror in order to ensure the safety of his image and keep separate that which he feared could be joined. Eve, however, joined them, made them miscible, utilizing her will.

A crested stream ran outward from the wells. It flowed westward and I could see, at great distance, a still pond, which it fed. The water contained in both stream and pond was streaked with unmixed liquid drawn from each well.

Not far from the pond I came upon a clearing in which stood a table. The table was of unhewn stone, its top surface ground smooth. Engraved on its surface were what appeared to be constellations, etched by instruments tracing geometric paths. There were no erasures, no indications that any-thing scratched was sanded free, that any layer of investigation was cleared before the next was commenced. The layers of information were intertwined in patterns unrelated to the hierarchy of surface application. The resulting complexity recalled the tendency of ill-fated communicative gestures falling beyond individual comprehension and succumbing to accusations of mysticism.

And then, in my path, a stumbling block.[12] A simple stone, cubic in shape, placed as an emblem on the ground. Enforced with mythical provenance by my companion, the stone donned the iconic identity of an early statue of Hermes without hands or feet. Cubic Hermes, poised in a gesture of solidity and stability, reflecting nature's generative power. A book lay on the side of the stone. It lay open and positioned as an embodiment of Hermes' missing shadow. It was large, old and composed of an endless number of very thin transparent pages. The stone, an emblem of uninformed nature, cast its shadow as prescient implication of informed matter, as a book.

A book forgotten? But not long forgotten. There were no signs of age or weathering.

A book left behind by a frequenter of the place? But surely one of this place would never leave the vulnerable so vulnerable.

22 I studied the inscribed pages but could not decipher the glyptic text. As I rested against the stone and contemplated the up-facing pages, a question entered my mind as if somehow inherent in the book's incongruous presence.

Was it an apple or a book that Eve tasted of? Did she take it with her or leave it open and only partially read? I closed my eyes in consideration. Resting my head on the stone I felt a vibration. Conquered by sleep, oblivious to the vibration's origin, I dreamed a dream of dreaming.

6

pursuing in darkness what was its task by light [13]

In the dream the Narrator asks Natura, What is the mystery I sense in this place?

> You sense the presence of the virtues and souls of mankind that have been banished from the world and dwell in the ether you found so moist.

And when were they banished?

> It was in their excommunication, while the world slept and dreamed.

And by whom were they banished?

> By human nature, which displaced them by unnatural passions and the choice of insensibility. They were collected in this place-without-shadows. Have you noticed the absence of shadows?

Is my shadow then waiting outside Zoar for my return?

> Your shadow is now within you. It is no longer external. You are now of darkness and of light. Your shadow is as mine, as you are now part of me.

Why excommunication?

Excommunication is the proof of man's insignificance in his relation to the fiction of his Creator, who could never accept him as His perfect reflection and is unaccepting of all that makes him human. Man, in imitation, excommunicates his fellow man as unacceptable, and bans him from communion, with not only other beings but with this very same Creator. Standing in as proxy for their Creator, human beings judge other human beings as unworthy of communion.

The souls of the excommunicated were released into the ether and collected there for a greater purpose. The world was once flooded and the end became the beginning in a man named Noah. No good came of this. The world was then set afire and Lot was allowed to walk away. Again, no good came of that, few lessons were learned and those learned were quickly forgotten. Now it will be the end by retraction, removal of that which is known as the soul, the light of the mind, the invisible force of life and creation. The informed matter of stuff of the world, the soul, will be retracted, not destroyed, just retracted. Retracted and assembled in the ether of Zoar.

And all else, the soulless, the uninformed matter?

As all of Creation's divisions will be withdrawn, only soulless uninformed matter will remain. All will be inanimate. Uninformed matter will be destined to await new breath.

When will this dissolution be completed? Will there be warnings?

It is a slow process, one that cannot be announced with simple warnings. A process that mankind helps along unknowingly on one hand but knowingly on the other. It is a process that actually began a long time ago and went unnoticed. It originated with the oppression of Eve. It surfaced at regular intervals in history. It is recalled as occurring in Egypt, then in Spain and its renaissance in Europe with inquisitions. It was recently noted as progressing scientifically in an event proclaimed as a war to end all wars. Reduced to an efficient scientific distillation it has been followed by the invention of weaponry that can vaporize whole popula-tions instantaneously. The scale-change of the process allows individuals the power of efficiency. Nothing further is needed to precipitate the completion of the filling firmament of Zoar. Mankind, humankind persists in its own destruction, persists in moving towards its completion. It is as if humankind has found itself unfit and is slowly insisting on suicide.

A sudden shifting of light frightened me awake to Natura's warnings. The faint resonating vibrations from the stone allowed my thoughts to refocus. I shook off the heaviness of sleep and consoled my trembling soul.

7

stone sermon: "bound to earth but full of heavenly thoughts" [14]

Sympathetic vibrations from Hermes' stone reverberated through the encompassing surround. Its origin remained a mystery. Walking a path I hoped would lead towards its source I noticed a bright sphere in the sky moving in the same direction.

In the distance a stone structure appeared.

The stones of the structure must be dry-set, I conjectured. I could hear the fragile joints vibrate and grind one against the other. The harmony of the vibrations must be in full concord, as the walls did not tumble under the strain. The inner chamber of the tower must then be symmetrical, I thought, not knowing why.

The luminous sky-born sphere seemed to be moving more quickly and began descending, revealing the silhouette of a tower by dropping behind it. The tower seemed empty of objects but overwhelmingly full of motion, the motion of air that produced sound. I stood listening to the harmonics being intoned as if from the grandest of instruments. As I listened the sound revealed itself more fully. Its detectable notes formed words, the words formed chords, the chords' phrases arranging themselves into a Sermon. It was a familiar Sermon expounding fundamental principles of infinite origins and futurity.

A Sermon by definition comes from a center, from a pulpiteer. I could account for three possible centers: that of the universe, that of its earth or that of my own containment reflected outward. Not able to distinguish which was its true center I chose to focus on the Sermon's principles rather than its mysteries.

The Sermon revealed the existence of four spheres rotating independently in a firmament, spheres that were outside the domain of the charted constellations of the stars, the moon, the sun and the earth. They were of mind, of soul, of cosmos and of supernal being. They travelled freely in their orbits, adjusting their paths in relation to one another as was required to maintain the harmony and concord of hum in the ether.

Floating in the flux between the spheres, systems for ordering and controlling the orbits had been constructed. Like nets cast upon the waters, they were cast upward into the firmament, accidentally catching birds, animals and angels indiscriminately. These illusory nets were woven and sometimes knotted in primitive patterns. Some knots were mathematically computed as a hymn to revered science and a geometrically constructed oblivion. Some were woven of magic and spells whose knots immobilized intruders at each crossing. Chants charmed other nets' tentacles into serpentine trances of intertwining convolutions. Often these nets were so dense they obliterated the spheres completely, but they never succeeded in preventing their motion.

The Sermon continued, revealing the places from which the nets were cast, narrated in bass and treble voices. These aural proclamations mixed with one another and also with those of earlier civilizations. Understanding became difficult, subtleties deepened and filled me with a great pain of familiarity, the familiarity perpetually suffered upon waking and understanding the momentous pattern of existence, which can on occasion cause paralysis of will.

Silence followed, a stilling that threatened to suck breath from the body. Then a vibrating after-tone resounded. It was part of the Sermon, serving as its signatory Amen, Amen, leading to, followed by, continuance.

A wavering stillness ensued. Voices from eternity past and future, released and hovering, mixed with small particles of incense and were gathered in the pocketed vaults above. Their multitude, collected between the crevices of the arching stone, were redrawn into motion with the reveille of organ notes, the shrill cry of a caller's voice and the blast from the horn of a sacrificial ram.

The Sermon conclusively celebrated a promised return, a victorious return, of the dispersed from the ether, then faded as the air regained composure. Relieved of tension, the tower's stones regained their secure repose one upon the other.

8

Following the Sermon's conclusion and the assurance of the stones' stability, I ventured into the tower. The absence of light was blinding, the floor uneven and unstable. The unevenness caused my feet to slip as I moved along grooves and impressions cut in different directions. As I adjusted to the dim dimensionlessness of the chamber I became aware of a maze set in the floor. Its pattern was intricate and moved in an inward as well as outward direction. I attempted to determine which direction to follow. I found there were other patterns, more subtly intertwined, competing in intricacy for my engagement. I stumbled, was tripped by my unschooled footing in its inability to follow labyrinthine contradiction. I retreated, exited the stone chamber and returned to the comfort of the brick wall's embrace. Viewing the tower from a more stable perspective I noticed a wearily thickening and irrefutable dusk transforming the landscape.

Remaining to discover Zoar's night invited contemplation. Remaining within its walls would confer upon me the role of inhabitant, who bears responsibility for choice of place coupled with responsibility for that place, an impropriety for a visitor. Not knowing what responsibility would require, choice obviated my departure. My journey now challenged navigation's ability to retrace paths taken in anticipation of a mythic return to comforting light. For a year and by day, drawn habitually, as if by trance, I would revisit Zoar's refuge.

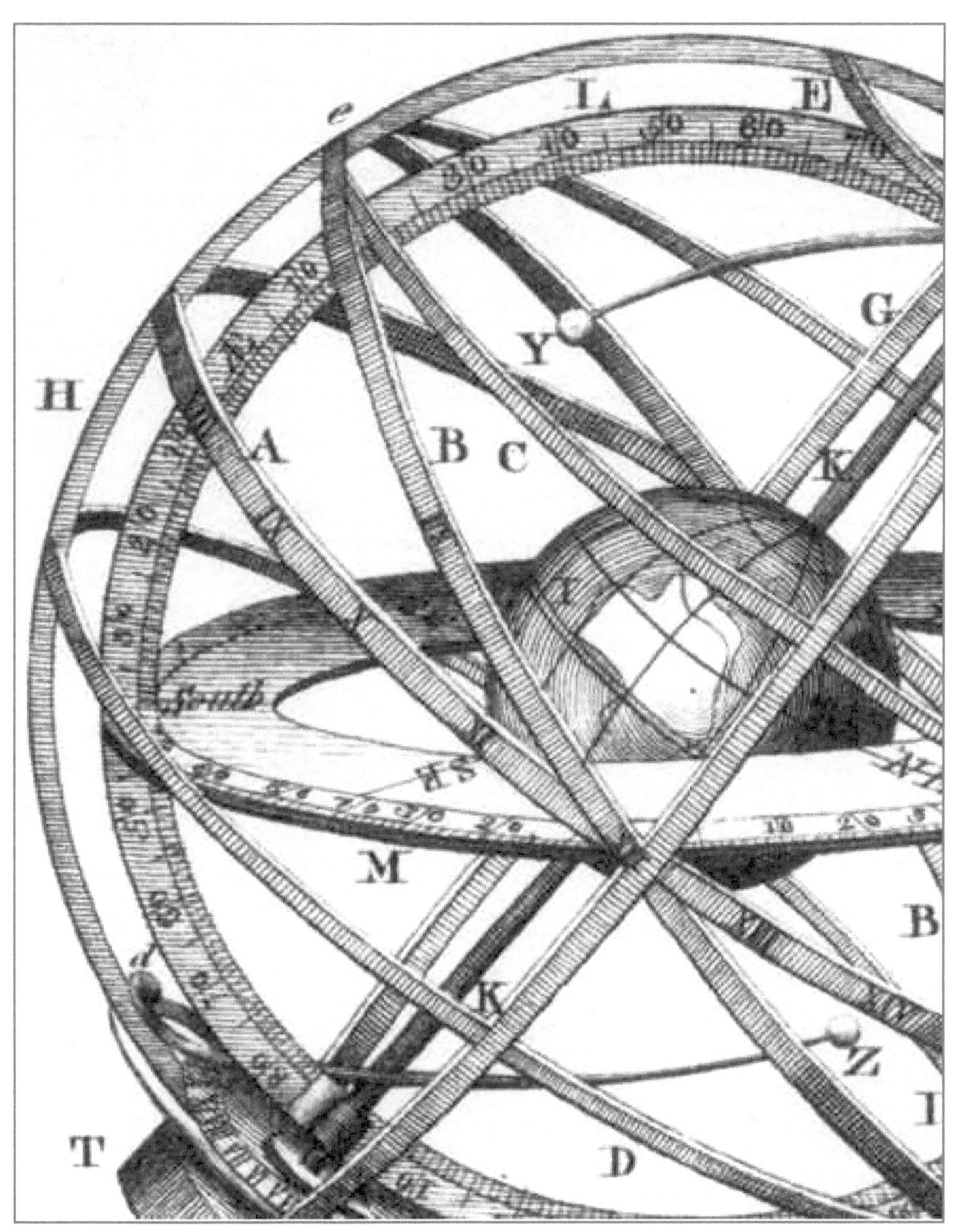

part two

9

in zenodochy [16] *they come to hear, they come that they may be heard.* [17]

Retiring from Zoar each day at the first sign of dusk allowed an unexpected discovery and welcome exchange. Taking a room at a nearby inn, the Zenodochy, I found myself in the company of a community of diverse Aspirants whose quests bore a striking resemblance to my own; aspirants, each of whom had found the ideas upon which the world was based unacceptable and had set out in search of alternatives. They sought a place from which to secure their momentum and ensure a timeless refuge that would offer respite.

Goaded by universal aspiration, they assembled in this contemplative *adytum* between excursions seeking coherence in the diversity of discovery. They shared gleanings from the detritus of things heard and seen, mixed with splintered fragments of landscape. Their collected revelations offered instances of accord that advocated, encouraged earnest continuation of their search.

Unconscious cerebration allowed recollection of an antiquated thought device, likened to concentricity's principles of the armillary sphere. The sphere's skeletal character allowed the idea of apparency in significant relationships between diversely expedient propositions. Strategically balanced, its orbit's unrestrained influence within constricting horizons and meridians offered a system of accountability. Earth, that infinite central point suspended in midair, thrusts its radial arms outward, first clutching then releasing its principles of action. The Aspirants understood that the centrality of the armillary sphere's earth influenced the interdependent actions of formed matter's bond with qualities of being. It was "*...not because the sun rises and sets, not because of the movement of the heavens, it is we ourselves...who rise and set.*" [18]

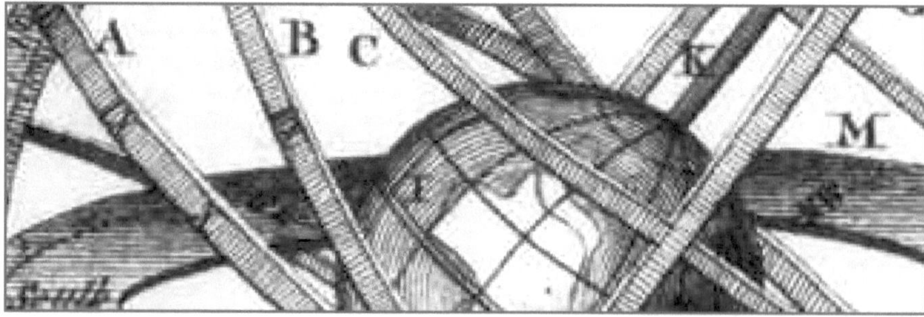

10

earth's extraction as raw material for elucidation, the one forms, the other is formed [19]

The Aspirants accepted the primacy of both the sun-dried brick, formed from earth's muddied *mortal* detritus, and the extracted stone, cut from the *immortal* body of earth's creation. They reasoned that although brick and stone shared origins of earthly extraction, one was formed by the hand and the other according to physical laws governing nature's defiance. Brick, they agreed, mimics the compressive resilience of stone but lacks fulfillment in aspiration for its longevity. Conversely, stone shares characteristic modularity in arcuated assemblage, but lacks the tensile immediacy of its

sun-dried brick competitor. With axiomatic reasoning it was concluded that as *brick* was to *stone* so was *mortality* to *immortality*. Zoar's brick walls protected its stone walls, as mortals protect that which is assumed to be immortal.

Is mortality the opposite of immortality? the initiates among them queried.

Mortality can exist without immortality but immortality is dependent on mortal desire for its existence. Mortality contains the immortal in its aspiration for longevity and perfection. The mortal creates the immortal as its extension, maintaining the anthropomorphic in reflex. Not opposite, they are however locked in a mesmerizing convergence, antagonized with imagined jealousies of pride, exception and belief.

The Aspirants understood stone as excavated, but the earth's muddied mortal detritus? What clay was that?

> Cyclically, in the continuum of creation, preservation and destruction, Natura was guaranteed ample matter with which to form futurity. In all manner of life she is the seed of creation, the bloom of preservation and the detritus of return. All manner of life instructs all other manner of life in her temporal involution. The earth's muddied mortal detritus supplied clay for brick. The clay offered the principle of regeneration for mortals' rebirth.

From dust to dust. A whisper and a nod of assent.

11
the knower within

"Men's minds are more deeply disturbed by what they do not see." [20]

The blooms of rose, lily and iris at Zoar's entry allude to Natura's persistence, her lure by desire.

Beyond the boundaries of ordinary knowledge the symbolist lure of destiny's path offering rose, lily and iris, is not readily apparent. On observation each bloom is found to have a unique geometry. The rose with five petals, the lily with six and the iris with seven petals gleaming like a rainbow. These numerical characteristics are occluded by the distracting magnificence of their blooms. Their qualities are known only for the ways they manifest themselves to the senses and not to their informed enumeration.[21]

The rose's five petals are reminders of the five elements and the five senses. The number Five is produced by the four cardinal points together with their center. The rose is symbolically the animator of centralized energy, inspiring outward passage, activating the five senses, coaxing energy to the hand to form primal matter.

The six-petaled lily signifies perfection in number and form. The world was made according to the number Six, in six days. The number Three is half of Six, Two a third, and its unit one-sixth. It is made equal to its parts and completed by them [3+2+1=6]. The lily goads precision in the transformation of thought into action.

The seven-petaled iris emphasizes the allusive measure of immortal beings' constancy. The number Seven is neither produced nor produces by number and remains immovable. The moon cycle occurs in increments of seven days, seven planets are counted, seven stars form the Bear that serves as a never-failing constellation for terrestrial orientation and navigation. Unmovable, unchangeable, Seven remains constant. The presence of the iris assures stability along the Aspirants' path.

On Zoar's path the rose beckons energy's ability to form, the lily wears the banner of precision in process and the iris offers assurance of resilience. Echoed da capo al fine, the five senses allow creative energy to emerge, the six-sided stone set before the seven planets etched on the table's surface, assures a precise unwavering and constant path of universal quest. Five, Six, Seven accede to the number Nine, the hermetic symbol of Truth. Nine, a triplication of the triplicate, 3x3=9, allusive in casual reception as 5+6+7=18, 1+8=9 or 5+6+7+18+9=45, 4+5=9. The blooms combined sequentially inform Truth's path.

If meaning is so occluded by distracting magnificence, how then are these signifiers to be communicated to the less informed? The Aspirants asked: Is the primitive stumbling block a reminder to the un-blinded of pedagogical responsibility to nature's unseen offerings?

One must always seek the virtues that can be found in the snares obstructing ones path. The open book under the shadow of Hermes' primitive stone expresses the necessity for the coexistence of the civilized state with its originating savage state, the informed with its progenitor, the uninformed. Copying the hovering constellations in primitive awe is a first gesture of the *awakening mind* (the Initiate).Transposing those constellations onto a surface, reflecting them in full conformity with understanding, requires the literacy of an *awakened mind* (the Aspirant). Configuring metaphoric constellations of imagined existence in the foundation of a rising tower is the maturing outcome of an *active mind* (the Adept). The primitive awe of the constellations bows to, and is replaced by, the literacy of civilized awe in gaining the ability of abstract thought. By the willingness to maturity these signifiers can come to be understood by the less informed.

Following the labyrinth was the pretense for a journey ensuring revelation of progress toward an imagined goal. Following the book's descriptive thought allowed revelation of progress toward an intellective goal. The pages' transparent universe held specks of floating symbolic matter that served to prove the hermetic axiom, that below is as that above or that seen is as that thought. The receptivity of the studying subject, the initiate, can ensure understanding by the less informed.

Will the world, devoid of division, imply a lessening of intelligence? With Natura absented, whence will wisdom and intelligence evolve? Whence will her catalytic beginnings, her gifts of seed, approach creation?

Natura bade a return to primitive origin. To a time before division, before naming and human intervention. A return, erasing that which urges mortals to maturity. Her proposition was simple: to join that which was divided. She, too, was a product of division and she, too, was ultimately lost to the chaos of the Tohu and Bohu. The question may be better phrased thus: Can Natura return as catalyst for beginnings? The answer is not predictable as nature and spirit, Natura and her soul, have no beginning.

12
what is time?

Evenings were spent tabulating the Aspirants' itineraries. Less and less time was spent visiting the place as more time was devoted to sorting its components. Lack of correlation between accounts became apparent. Incongruity grew to staggering proportions and could be quelled only by the addition of newly agreed-upon categories. With little in the way of correlation, a richly discordant communal voice formed, formed as if inherent in and originating from the nature of the place sought. Agreement, or lack of it, did not curb or limit aspiration but rather served to fuel its momentum.

Establishing the actual location of the sought-after place was a major focus for the Aspirants, who in their explorations came upon common places of diverse descriptions. Groups formed. Believing they were on the verge of discovery, the anticipation of the Aspirants grew with propelling forcefulness. Chronology was considered a possible common denominator in the Aspirants' attempt to integrate discoveries with sequential occurrence.

Underscored with a notion of linear time, their use of chronology suffered complication. What was time?

The Aspirants' attempt at objective accounting eventually lost its usefulness. The propensity to assess discoveries by exercise of chronological list-making proved unproductive. Poised beside the voice of narration, objective chronology was found to be lifeless. Wordsmiths were called upon for remedy. Formulation of a less literal accounting was sought to ensure preservation of the excitement that had first enticed exploration.

Artificers were consigned to further enhance their method. They were known to have experience in balancing chronology with narration. The Artificers, by trade, assembled material in a chronologically compelling process, responding to the laws of gravity and equilibrium, attending to those temporal issues of setting in place an upper level securely on a foundation. Simultaneously they gave voice to the transformation of thought within impending space by naming it to its perceptible configuration.

13
life processes as motif

...nothing is more delightful than to possess well-fortified sanctuaries, serene, built-up by the teachings of the wise, from which you may look down from its heights and behold all those wandering abroad seeking a path of life. [22]

Mediating incongruent aspiration, the Initiates composed Truth's fiction by balancing rhetoric with purposeful action. Common descriptive elements depicting life's processes as motifs were found within their individually revealed well-fortified sanctuaries. Differentiations' apparency arose with the understanding that they could not communicate in any other language than their own.

In all the descriptive motifs there were Gates encircling Courts containing Temples soliciting Refuge. Before each Gate, a group sat in reverence. Beyond each Court, a vast and empty Desert, a no-man's land, beyond which a Garden flourished. There were no apparent signs of attempts to enter or cross the Desert to reach the Gardens. No conscious need evoked the will to challenge that seemingly parched place. The Temples were raised as universally inclusive markers of the evolution of the symbolic representation of the spiritual.

Each motif, although incorporating common elements, was unique in its configuration and rite. To fulfill the needs of its conjurors it was situated so as to mask and visually obliterate the presence of the others. Each place revealed its unique truth and intent. Each offered the humbling historic Garden as backdrop.

14
first motif

Of the places claimed to have been revealed this was the most primitive. Its walls were in sad disrepair. They had been constructed of brick with a mortar mixture of blood and sand. The additive blood was believed to en-sure the greatest of bonds, far outreaching the bond of language. The walls' fragility, their apparent deterioration, and consequent impending failure, was believed to be due to the mixture of bad blood with that which was considered to be good or pure blood.

According to description, there was a ritual practiced here which com-menced with the choosing of a Sacrificer, who would render sacred that which was to be considered sacred. It was then propitiated with offerings of such things as incense, animals, innocent beings, candles, money or those thought to be allied with the angel of darkness. The noblest offering, and the most misunderstood, seemed to be the voluntary offering of a celebrant's own body with self-mortification, ritual bleeding or starvation.

> *...of these humble and august souls, who dare to dwell on the very brink of the mystery, waiting between the world which is closed and heaven which is not yet open, turned towards the light which one cannot see, possessing the sole happiness of thinking that they know where it is, aspiring towards the gulf, and the unknown, their eyes fixed motionless on the darkness, kneel-ing, bewildered, stupefied, shuddering, half lifted at times by the deep breaths of eternity...*

Each one of them in turn made what they call reparation. The reparation in the prayer (or offering) for all the sins, for all the faults, for all the dissensions, for all the violations, for all the inequities, for all the crimes committed on earth....[23]

15
second motif

If the first place was the most primitive, it can be said that the second was the most frenzied. Those frequenting this place were worked up into a state of high excitement. That their temple was built of mail armor and metallic plate was enough to excite the simplest of minds among them. There was yet more to this state of euphoria: It was believed that their temple contained a Speaking Head. To believe is to trust; to trust is to take, to accept, in good faith that which cannot be seen, understood or proved. Accepted, as the child accepts the mother's milk, as the sheep follow the shepherd, in trust... to trust the words of the other, the other whose role has been decreed.

The Head could not be described. It had never been seen. Entry to the temple was allowed only to select individuals. Those claiming to have been allowed entry never approached the Head too closely. They claimed that one could not look directly into its eyes nor could its visage be directly engaged. Those who could hear it could listen. It was said to be able to sing, speak, warn, advise and prophesy. Its existence could be argued, never proved.

The Head was as impressive as the oracle of the ancient Greeks. Speculation surrounding it was comparable to that of ancient times as related to consciousness after decapitation. Historical confirmation had inspired speculation that located the soul and intellect on the inner landscape of the brain.

There was no reference to a garden or desert. I inquired about these absences and received an unexpected response.

Curiosity is a dangerous position from which to question, they scolded.

How, after discovering this Head, should they look further? This was enough for them, they explained, as they were but mere mortals, mere mortals in the presence of unquestionable phenomena.

They called upon the Head for assistance and assurance. They had no need to look beyond it and no need to question those in indirect communication with it. If the Head did not instruct them to question, did not hint at the existence of unseen gardens or deserts, did not instruct them to search for what they did or did not see or hear…then there was nothing more, nothing beyond or before consideration.

16
third motif

In a dark corner of the inn sat those who had seen nothing and spoke only of what they had heard in a forecourt before a gate. Nothing had been seen. Chants had stolen their hearts, blinding them to everything else.

Theirs was a place of music chanted by blind singers. Blind singers were the only ones both spiritual and worldly enough to sing the compositions. Their transmission reflected the limitless vision of internal image apparent only in the realm of the soul.

The chants were recited, tonally perfect, with the understanding that any imperfection would render the entire composition invalid. If learned incorrectly or recited confusedly, getting words and meter mixed up, it was possible that the very thing to be corrected or protected by the vocal composition would be made worse. The practiced monophonic forms of vocalization were for them the truest form of entreaty.

The chanters' training was rigorous. It was work induced by perfection, or the aspiration for perfection, that was entirely internal to each candidate. It was work for the chanters to do within themselves to reach the desired precision. Some believed it was this compulsion that blinded the chanters, that they became frozen on their darkened path, masked in a deep tonality that the mortal step could not follow. The loss of the eye, superstition fearfully suggested, is sometimes accompanied by the loss of the soul. It was not so much the loss of the soul that was feared but its captivity and imprisonment.

17
fourth motif

The fourth place could more accurately be called a gate. It was a site of celebration. Here the participants gathered to sing. They sang praises. They sang in the hope that the Gate would open the Arch of Heaven to them. They stood before the Gate and sang its praises.

The Gate was sung to with such great praise that it itself became that which was believed to be the essence of what was sought. It grew in importance in their minds and became the most praised, the highest representation of what it was they cherished, aspired to cherish or believed worthy of its cherished unquestionability.

Replicas of the Gate were molded in miniature and could be found in the homes of the participants or worn on small chains hanging over the heart. The Gate became for them a true firmament and was translated as such in their hymns. Philosophers warned of the dangers inherent in praise and magnification of the adored, or yearned for, as becoming filled with the spirit of pride and vainglory. Warnings unheeded, the Gate increased in vainglory.

18
fifth motif

The fifth group of Aspirants was made up of children. Their place was determined less by metaphors of Gates, Courts and Places of Refuge and more by its inhabitants' relationships to one another. They were not conjurers. They lived a fluid world, unfixed, imagined, ever-changing in present time, reflecting their individuation. Listening to adults' accounts of places revealed convinced them that those accounts were a retelling of old well-known stories. This pleased them, as they felt that the adults were involved in matters that were familiar to them.

The children's descriptions of their place were sometimes endless in repetition, often retold several times before overcoming troublesome understanding or conclusion. They spoke slowly, patiently and listened in silent earnestness. I learned that it never rained in their place, or perhaps, I thought, they never visited when it did rain. There were wells from which to drink and berries to eat. There were secret places and haunted dreams. There was a Storyteller, someone from whom music was emitted, and others whose identity was less clear. One day, they related, they met two very young children in a garden.

The first seemed to be more of a storybook figure than an ordinary child. It dug like a squirrel, ate like a rabbit, made sounds like birds and seemed to crawl about, at times, on all fours. When first approached, the child froze in place like a deer, listened and then dashed off. Over time it stayed still longer and longer, allowing approach and even proximity, accepting small bits of muffin from picnic handkerchiefs, smelling everything first.

Adam was the name given to the other child, who seemed identical in appearance and age but more outward in gesture and understanding, who spoke clearly and seemed more like the visiting children. It came as a great surprise when it was revealed that they both bore the name Adam. Although they shared the same name each signaled variation in origin and futurity.

The two Adams looked alike. Not that they were twins: one seemed a duplicate of the other. Which was the original and which the copy could be argued. One seemed more perfect than the other in versatility and sophistication. Could an original be more perfect than the copy? Is the first an attempt and the second its perfection?

The Adams shared similar form and name but each had a separate and unique being. This was apparent in the way each could see. The first Adam seemed to stare openly into a distance beyond average sight, beyond life with nothing blocking or deflecting vision. There was no need to focus or refocus, to squint when looking at things close or things at a distance, things detailed or things textured. There was a peering out without focusing on anything in particular in an attempt, it seemed, to find an aperture through which to spring into an unknown, always on the verge of moving forward towards an elusive existence. Was this an attempt to outsmart prey—or an undisciplined shadow?

The other Adam was different. Movement was not reliant on instinct. Movement was precipitated by a contemplative dimension that seemed unfathomable, bottomless. There was light in her eyes that seemed to imply a space behind them. A light that overpowered all else about her. The children thought she was looking back, back into inner space, seeking the aperture that would allow her exit before the picture plane. Her eyes were blue and were as clear as they were piercing. When speaking with her the children tended not to look her in the eye. They were not always sure whether she was looking out or looking in. *Out* was defensible. *In* brought on fears of being drawn into an inescapable abyss behind her gaze.

19

other inhabitants

The children spoke of a Tower that was made of the whitest stone. The Adams believed that fire was locked within each stone, causing the Tower's white glow. Perhaps, they proposed it had been made from stones fallen from the moon.

The Tower was poised in a protective gesture that attracted immediate focus. It had been named the Protector by the Adams. Someone named the Protector was its prime inhabitant and lived either between the walls or in its hollow chamber, standing sentinel. That there was a Protector seemed logical. Surely, small children could not survive unguided and alone, their civilized and perhaps instructed condition bore witness to that.

And what did the Protector look like? Like the Adams? I asked. No, I was assured, it looked like the Tower. The facades of the Tower were marked with patterns of openings, doors and windows that gave the impression of a face. This anthropomorphism duplicated itself in the Protector's face or was it vice versa? The Protector was described as strong. He wore long cloaks and knew how to charm serpents. Justice was important in its actualization but there was no certainty as to how it was balanced. The Adams described the Protector as ever-present and allied to no particular being or cause.

And what does the Protector do? the Adams were asked.

> The Protector maintains its condition. It does so by assuming the role of Chronologer, protecting the continuity of events by pinning them to language. The Protector records nothing in writing. That is left to others, who record what they think this chronology contains.

The Adams deftly inverted our conversation, turning it from the symmetry of question and answer to a mode more allied with storytelling, with answers preceding questions. They spoke in propositions that prompted, encouraged, complex and varied questions. For them the purpose of storytelling was not about proof or disproof, but about meaning and intent. The Adams knew thousands of stories. The children responded in awe. In awe, not at the number of stories, but at the multitude of variation of one story.

As the children shared the Adams' stories with me, I wondered how they had learned to form them so adeptly. Could they read? and if so, who had taught them this constructive currency? Did they have a teacher? I inquired one day.

Yes, they had at least two, they assured me, and they learned more than reading.

20

an arch, a bridge, an abyss

Within the enclosing walls of Zoar inscribed arches of differing depth served as a gateway. The space below the arches belonged to its children. There was a sweet sound contained within this defined domain. It was the echo of the first child's voice continuously reverberating. Hidden in the floral motifs decorating this aurality a phrase repeated itself endlessly. It could be heard accompanied by children's giggling.

Life without children is like an arch resting on one pillar, a bridge ending in an abyss.[24]

Of all the inhabitants, the children were by nature the freest and could be found everywhere. They played in the landscape and made the acquaintance of visitors. Their education began with a Progenitor and was completed by a Storyteller and a Music Teacher.

21
trivium [25]

The children were at first occupied solely with seeing and hearing. It was as if an insatiable desire to see and to hear had seized them, and they enjoyed this pleasure, which no one could interrupt. Their education began with the learning of rhymes and divinations. They were never to forget the repeated lullabies and finger-toe enumerations. The counting-out or telling-out rhymes were most important, and as soon as they learned to accept what was to be their fate, when the lot would fall upon them, they were ready to accept all other lessons that would occupy, perhaps challenge, their lives. From then on, words and sounds for them gained meaning.

The Storyteller spoke with them first. Her stories were geometric and served to sow seeds of equality and just proportion: the geometry of language, by means of a balance of contemplation with speculation, implanted an admiration for justice in their souls. [26]

In her stories there were no punitive spirits, no avenger, no ungenerous watching eye. She did not leave fear to curb her charges and enforce discipline. The Storyteller did not protect the children from stories full of evil or undue punishment. She told her stories in such a way that within each character, each act or event, the redeemable could be read. She allowed each listener to determine what was good, what imaginary and what real. Her charges freely misheard, as they would later misread and mis-tell, in order to ensure inner peace. They knew they were free to re-form a story to correct confusion or instill balance in the world about them.

The Storyteller lived in a tower. She was always present and always spinning asides to explanations. When not telling stories, she would weave on a large loom, adjusting patterns, motifs and compositions as her stories found their place in the warp under her fingers. The handwork, the details of the weave, were formed with the same intricacy as the characters and events populating her stories. The warp of her great loom stretched around its beam and back, passing only once through her hands to receive the shuttle or knot of the bobbin. It then continued out from her tower, across the ethereal screen of the horizon intersecting adjacent towers. A path of colorful patterns could be seen from afar and the children could always look upward into the weft and read its linear throw of lines. The words did not dissipate or vanish in the atmosphere. The ribbons of woven color led across the sky and were eventually drawn into and under the base of a distant tower.

The Storyteller feared her stories were being buried in a subterranean world. She imagined that they became part of a sea of data, of artificial intelligence under the heap of distant towers, with little hope of redemption. To counter this fear she taught the children to keep her stories free from this muting destiny. She taught them that to keep the stories alive, they must be kept on children's lips and uttered. She made each child promise to tell at least one of the stories each day and to exact the same promise from the listener, with an oath of secrecy as to their goal. In exchange for this promise she agreed to tell them stories until the end of time, knowing full well that time never ends.

The Storyteller lived with the Music Teacher. Their cohabitation was a joining of orbital narration with metronymic time. As neither restricted the other, they shared a matrimonial allegory of equilibrium.

22
quadrivium [27]

The Music Teacher spoke to them next and was responsible for the remainder of their education. He taught them what was harmonious. He rejected all that was out of tune, guiding that which was discordant to concord. His lessons began with history. He explained that the sound of notes existed before words and that there were once stories whose words were used for their sound rather than their meaning. It was in the relationship between the sounds that meaning evolved and became interchangable.

He admitted that he did not know the specific scientific origin of sound, nor the origin of the ordering of sounds into words or language. In this matter he deferred to the *Popul-Vuh*:

> ...when men found their first seats too narrow, the old god resolved to spread them over the whole earth, and give to each his own language. For this purpose he placed a cauldron of water on the fire and commanded the different beings to

approach and select for themselves the sounds they favored, which were uttered by the singing water in its confinement. [28]

The Music Teacher taught variations of the origin of sound as *Musica Ficta*. One day, speculation led him to propose that in the separation of the waters, on the second day of beginnings, when the sea was separated from the land, the first sound was heard. It was the sound of the waters crying out in joy, humbled by the ebb and flow of their new boundary choreographed in a cosmic trance with the moon. This cry, he continued, deafened the universe for millennia. In sympathy, the stars and planets circled the earth in a frenzy, whirring through the vastness. To this day the sound of their whirring can be heard by a select few, ensuring memory of that first cry.

Why they asked, why would the sound of water crying out generate the sympathy of stars and planets?

> Sound is like the flowing motion of both the sea below and the heavens above, of their turbulence, their bursting inner life and intertwining currents. It is as free as the sea in its expanse and as free as the heavenly spheres in their infinite outward flow. Sound holds the essential chord of a symphonic score of empathic motion. It is the intermediary between that which is above and that which is below, and prescribes the sympathetic pulse of throbbing life. Likewise the infinite flow of birth's first outcry marks the setting of life's pulsating metronome.

The Music Teacher required two spaces for instruction. The first was called a practice room. It was not only for the practice of music, it also served as a space for the practice of all other things requiring repetition. The second was a space found within an object, a body or a musical instrument and took on three distinct forms that covered the full range of sound. There was a vibrating column of air, a resonating chamber vaulted with vibrating strings and the space of a pulsatile shock of a body of matter in violent collision with another.

Each child chose a space, then shaped metal, stone, wood and sometimes string to refine clarity in the manipulation of the trembling air. Every column of air, every vibrating string, every pulse was unique, unique but in concord with the others. As they clearly uttered their notes, becoming successful architects of the space of their sound, their formal education found its completion. Their hands were instruments of the will, the Music Teacher taught, and sound was the instrument of the soul. He taught that with the construction of the vibrating columnar voice, coupled with the pulsatile shock of thought, the quivering viscera of the soul could be given occurrence.

23
twice born

At first in the dark silent womb we are like fish, breathing through water, fed without tasting through connectivity, sharing the life blood of maternal wealth. Passing out of this restless state and through the cervical gate everything changes. Discharged, we are drawn downward by gravity. With chest compressed, air rushes in to fill the nostrils and expand the empty lungs. Lips forcefully open to exhale a transformed breath. We cry out. That cry startles the eyes open to allow light entry. We taste. We swallow. We touch and are touched. We inhale the borrowed breath of corporality, of mortality. As the breath of life rushes in, it inadvertently charges a pulsating metronome. This pulsating timepiece, the heart, awakens the soul, commencing memories' continuance. By metamorphosis we are said to be twice-born, once to the finite and corporeal world of mortality and once to the world of the infinite and incorporeal soul.

A soul is always a soul. It is born into the world through the body. The body is of change, the soul constant. The body grows. The soul does not. It is already grown. Grown over generations and placed in recurrent time. It was the Ba or the Ka for the Egyptians, never spoken of as young Ba or young Ka, but understood as ageless. In ancient Greece it was called the genius and belonged to individual families. The family genius was born and reborn into its generations, never lost or damaged if conception was astrologically correct.

A soul can check the body before the body has a chance to check it. The possibilities are twofold: to join together that which is separate, the body with the soul, or to separate that which is joined, the body from the soul. To be strengthened by division or weakened by union, beset with conflict or unity, enmity or twinship, autonomy or unanimity.

The condition of the child as all soul is natural. For the adult to be all soul is different. With the child the soul and the body are at peace. The soul is free, the body is free. This is not so for the adult. Why does it open the child but cause the adult to close in upon itself?

24
sixth motif

It is raining in Zoar. The children will not be seen. It is raining and one can hear the rustling of the forest clearly. One can hear the birds call from under their wings, their voices amplified by the water's particular surface. It is on these misted days that the Recluse receives visitors and whispers to the Storyteller. She is a former Storyteller.

She walks in Natura's visceral landscape and carries a lantern partially covered by the folds of her cloak. When finding the serpent in her path, she charms it into twining itself around her staff. Recognition of her reflection in a well causes her to close her cape tightly. Its blackness shimmers with the depth of a mercurial mirror. With her cape closed, her light is hidden, but not extinguished. This inner light enhances the darkness of her appearance. She walks as a pillar of hidden light.

She is more light than matter, more soul than flesh. Her lantern is a constant beacon to those journeying not far behind. She holds it high and shows the way. Her silence lends alluvial purity to her imagined being. She is envied her solitude. Speaking, her voice compresses reflective thought. She is allocated scarce time in which to reveal her explications, insight or knowledge of her ascent. The paucity of those moments burdens her with entombing lament.

She asks, What is this about? Echo, hidden behind shrubs at the probing well, gives response:

> *About*, she echoes, *about* incommunicability, *incommunicability* of meaning, of merit and of inclination of the knowledge of life processes.[29]

They nod and she walks on. She is satisfied. She has found the refuge she had hoped to meet at a crossroad in the desert. A refuge offering respite. It is inherent in her destiny. Her personal self is shed, surrendered to experience, and replaced with the conscious understanding that all volition is universal rather than personal…. It is of yourself that the tale is told.

Knowing how grievous it is for the soul to be without a protector, she draped herself with the mortal fabric of Zoar's walls. Shielded with necessity's cloak she entered Zoar's refuge. Cloaked with the mortal bricks' embrace of stones' allusion, Zoar entered her.

Although *reclausa*, she is not alone. She is part of a cosmic urge to freedom accompanied by the eternal laughter of children and Echo's beseeching replies. When entering a city of refuge one is freed. When becoming a city of refuge one is indebted to those who in aspiration follow.

25
reclaudere

She watches, watches silently. She listens and nods from time to time knowingly or unknowingly. She drifts through vacant rooms, acknowledges uncleared tables, festivals' preparations, untidy desks… and places rose petals on tear-stained pillows.

THE REQUIEM[30] **ZOAR**[31]

epilogus

The portrait of this imaginary journey is meant to heighten the recurrence
of the soul's search for Truth, sealed and hidden in a sought-after refuge.
The infinite and modified variety of human preferences uncover Truth and
its struggle in distinction from other Truth.

vrw

glosses

0. *scordatura* [It.]
Baker, Theodore, *Pocket Manual of Musical Terms*, Intentional tuning of a stringed instrument in an irregular manner to obtain special effects. 1933

1. *emigratus* [L.] emigration.
Funk and Wagnalls, New Standard Dictionary, 1934

2. "That which is below is as that which is above..."
Yates, Francis A., *Giordano, Bruno and the Hermetic Tradition*, 1964

3. "...be the bearer of the seedling...and return in exultation, a bearer of sheaves...."
Psalm 126, *Artscroll Tehillim*, 1988

4. "it is of yourself the tale is told"
Horace, *Satirae 69*

5. "earth's false dreams"
Virgil, *Ecloga 893*

6. "ghosts of disappeared cities...."
Lord Dunsany, *A Dreamer's Tales*, 1910

7. "Behold now.......city called Zoar"
Genesis 19. 20-23

8. "a fossil of fish life...."
Muller, Max, *Chips from a German Workshop*, 1869

9. Natura complains about the disorderly behavior of informed matter. Ibid.

10. *gilgal* [Heb.] repeated action driven by the wind.
Hebrew English Lexicon of the Bible, 1975

11. Eve bowed her head before Adam. Her second, her outer voice proclaimed, "Not my will, but thine." Her first inner voice protests. "My will is illusive, but it is free although hidden, it is reflected and inverted by the mask of thy will."
Milton, John, *Paradise Lost*

12. "...nor put a stumbling block before the blind...."
Leviticus 19.14

13. "…pursuing in darkness what was its task by light.…"
Petronius, *Fragmenta 121*

14. "…bound to earth but full of heavenly thoughts"
Quintilian, *Institutio oratoria, I*

15. "…beyond which one cannot find a resting place.…"
Horace, *Satirae 106*

16. "…they come to hear, they come that they may be heard.…"
Ovid, *Ars amatoria*, tr. Frazer, James G., *Golden Bough*

17. *zenodochy* [Gr.] place to receive guests

18. "…not because the sun rises and sets, not because of the movement
of the heavens, it is we ourselves who rise and set.…"
Seneca, *Thyestes VII, ii, 2*

19 "…as raw material for elucidation; the one forms, the other is formed.…"
Quintillian, *Institutio oratoria, XIX, 3*

20. "…Men's minds are more deeply disturbed by what they do not see.…"
Caesar, *Commentarii de Gallico, VII, 84*

21. Formulations of numerical myth were based on the belief that man could
replicate the perceived order of the universe, of divine hierarchy which
existed in the universe for the very purpose of imitation. Things created
required arrangement, and Number was akin to arrangement. A cosmology
of Number evolved.

> The number One produced all numbers. Perceived in it and as-
> cribed to it were the nature and appellation of the limit. It was
> the point. Two produced the image of matter being divided, two
> parts or duality. It was represented by the line which goes from
> behind forward. Three became the first image of the solid body.
> It could be divided by dimension. It became unity as a solution
> to duality. Four was the foundation of creation, four elements out
> of which the universe was made: earth, air, water and fire, within
> which the four seasons turn. Five represented the five forms of
> matter and the senses. It was produced by the four cardinal
> points together with their center. Six was considered the first per-
> fect number. The world had been made according to the number
> Six in six days, the number Three being half of it, Two a third

and its unit a sixth of it and therefore made equal to its parts and completed by them. Seven was the measure of mortal being. That which is neither produced nor produces remains immovable. Immovable were the Elders, Rulers or Creators. It was the number free of motion and accident. The moon cycle in increments of seven days, the seven planets counted, seven stars forming the Bear who served as a never failing constellation on communication and terrestrial orientation. Eight was produced by 2 x 4 but produced no other number. Nine was the triplication of the triplicate and the symbol of Truth and the perfect number of hermetic tradition. Ten was the goal, as a return to unity: ten digits, ten commandments by which to measure all things.

22. "...But nothing is more delightful than to possess well-fortified sanctuaries, serene, built up by the teachings of the wise, from which you may look down from its heights and behold all those wandering around seeking a path of life...."
Lucretius, *De Rerum Natura, 7*

23. "... of these humble and august souls, who dare to dwell on the very brink of the mystery, waiting between the world which is closed and heaven which is not yet open, turned towards the light which one cannot see, possessing the sole happiness of thinking that they know where it is, aspiring towards the gulf, and the unknown, their eyes fixed motionless.... Each one of them in turn made what they call reparation. The reparation in the prayer (or offering) for all the sins, for all the faults, for all the dissensions, for all the violations, for all the inequities, for all the crimes committed on earth."
Hugo, Victor, *Les Miserables*

24. "...an arch resting on one pillar, a bridge ending in an abyss...."
Muller, op. cit.

25. trivium
Mackey's *Encyclopedia of Freemasonry*: Three Paths of learning; place where three roads meet; grammar, rhetoric and logic; of the seven liberal arts.

26. paraphrased description of education
Wells, H.G., *Kings Crown*

27. quadrivium
Mackey's *Encyclopedia of Freemasonry*: Four Paths of learning; place
where four roads meet; arithmetic, geometry, music, astronomy; of the
seven liberal arts.

28. *Popul-Vuh, Sacred Book of the Quidie Indians of Guatemala*

29. "it is about the incommunicability of meaning, merit and inclination of
the knowledge of life processes...."
Case, Paul F., *Key to the Wisdom of the Ages*

30. requiem
Funk and Wagnalls: rest, repose, peace

31. *Zoar* [Heb.] insignificant, small

illustrations

author

v regi weile is an architect, artist and writer. Her contemplative studies have focused on the inherent belief patterns concealed in the constructed or literary forms of architecture.

v regi weile is a practicing architect, a former professor of architecture at The Irwin S. Chanin School of Architecture of The Cooper Union and was a guest lecturer at many national and international educational institutions.

v regi weile was born in New York City, attended the High School of Music and Art and Pratt Institute School of Architecture. She now resides in the quietude of the North Fork of Long Island.

9 780615 966175